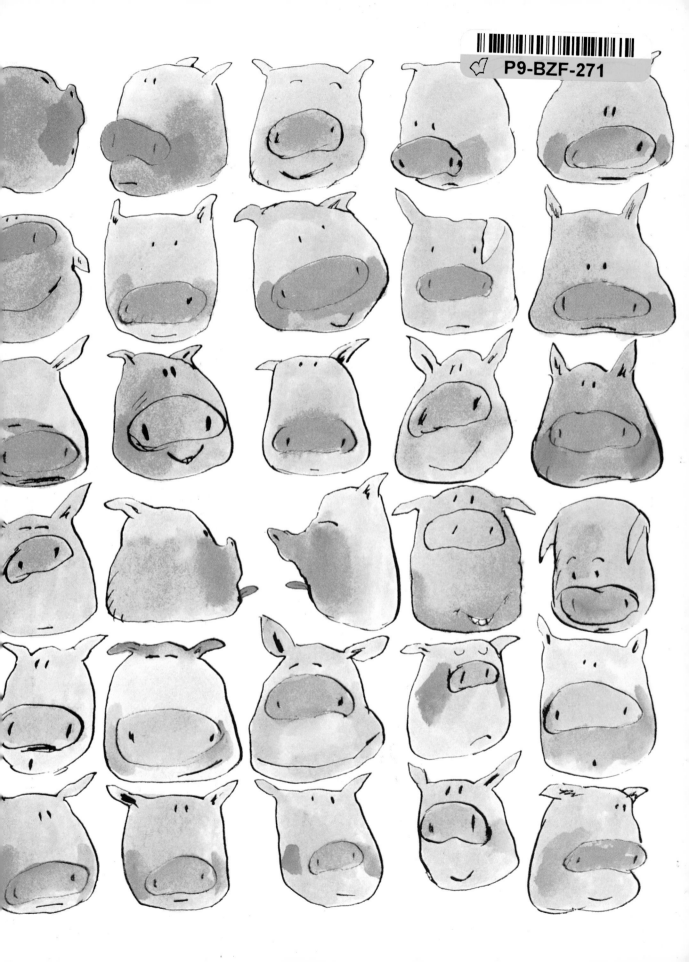

THE HUTCHINSON
BOOK OF
PIG
TALES

A COLLECTION OF PIGGY STORIES AND POEMS

HUTCHINSON
LONDON SYDNEY AUCKLAND JOHANNESBURG

First published in 2000

1 3 5 7 9 10 8 6 4 2

First published in the United Kingdom in 2000 by
Hutchinson Children's Books
The Random House Group Limited
20 Vauxhall Bridge Road, London SW1V 2SA

Random House Australia (Pty) Limited
20 Alfred Street, Milsons Point, Sydney
New South Wales 2061, Australia

Random House New Zealand Limited
18 Poland Road, Glenfield
Auckland 10, New Zealand

Random House South Africa (Pty) Limited
Endulini, 5A Jubilee Road, Parktown 2193, South Africa

The Random House Group Limited Reg. No. 954009

www.randomhouse.co.uk

A CIP catalogue record for this book is available
from the British Library

ISBN: 0 09 176934 5

Printed in Singapore

CONTENTS

Colin McNaughton

BOO!

THROUGH THE DARK, dark streets of the dark, dark town, Preston (the Masked Avenger) sneaks . . .

"BOO!" says Preston
the Masked Avenger

and he disappears into the night.

9

Slinking through the shadows,
Preston the Masked Avenger spies
Billy the Bully, his next victim . . .
"BOO!" says Preston the Masked Avenger
and he disappears into the night.

Cat-like, Preston the Masked Avenger slides through
the darkness until he reaches the
school-house where his teacher
is working late . . .

"BOO!"
says Preston the
Masked Avenger
and he disappears
into the night.

Next, the super-hero comes to Mr Wolf's house.

"Boo!" says Preston the Masked Avenger very quietly and he sneaks right past.

"I may be a super-hero," says Preston, "but I'm not daft!"

And he disappears into the night.

13

Preston the Masked Avenger lies in wait for the
greatest villain in the universe – his dad.
"BOO!" says Preston the Masked Avenger
and he disappears into the night.

(At least, he would have done if his dad hadn't grabbed him first.)

"Preston!" says Preston's dad. "I've had complaints about you from all over town. You're a naughty little pig."

Preston the Unmasked Avenger is sent to his room without any supper.

Suddenly!

"BOO!" says Preston's dad.
"That'll teach you to go around scaring people."

But it doesn't.

Holly Keller

Geraldine's Baby Brother

GERALDINE PUT ON HER EARMUFFS and sat behind the big chair.
"Why are you wearing earmuffs in the house?" Uncle Albert
asked when he saw her.

"So I can't hear *it*," Geraldine snapped, and she pointed to
Willie's basket.

"But I thought you wanted a baby brother," Uncle Albert said.

"Not *that* one," Geraldine grumbled, and she turned the page
without looking up.

The doorbell rang and
Willie started to cry.

Mama came out of the kitchen.

Aunt Bessie came down from the
bedroom, and Papa got up from the sofa.

It was Mrs Wilson to see Mama. She had
a big present for Willie and a present for
Geraldine, too.

"And where *is* Geraldine?" Mrs Wilson asked while she was tickling Willie.

"Nowhere," Geraldine snarled from behind the chair.

So Mrs Wilson left Geraldine's present on the table.

Willie cried all morning. Aunt Bessie picked him up and patted him.

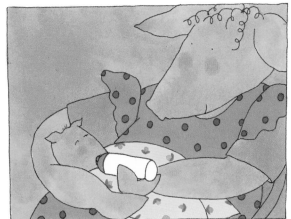

Mama gave him a bottle,

and Papa carried him all
around the house.

Uncle Albert made funny faces.
But at lunchtime Willie was
still crying.

"Oh, dear," Mama said suddenly.
"Where's Geraldine? She must
be starving."

Geraldine was in her room.

"How about a sandwich?" asked Mama.

Geraldine turned away. "I don't see you."

Mama sat down on the edge of the bed, but Geraldine slid off the other side and walked out of the door.

Late in the afternoon Geraldine came into the kitchen. "I'm going to take my bath now, and then I'm going to bed."

"That's nice, dear," Mama said quickly over her shoulder. Willie was still screaming.

Papa was waiting outside the bathroom when Geraldine opened the door.

"Aunt Bessie made lasagne for dinner, Geraldine, especially for you."

"Not hungry," Geraldine grumbled, and she disappeared into her room.

In the middle of the night Geraldine heard Willie moving around in his basket. She got out of bed and marched across the hall to the nursery.

"No more crying," she said sternly. Willie looked at her and yawned.

"I mean it," she added.

Willie rubbed his face and stuck out his tongue.
"You're weird," she said.

Willie stuffed his hand into his mouth and sneezed, and Geraldine
laughed because she couldn't help it. But Willie didn't cry.

Geraldine stuck her fingers in her ears, and he still didn't cry.

She turned on the light, and Willie gurgled. So she sat in the rocking
chair and read him some stories.

In the morning Mama found them both asleep. "Breakfast, anyone?" she whispered.

Geraldine opened her eyes. She was *really* hungry. "Can I give Willie his bottle?" she asked, and she patted Willie's head.

"How nice," Mama said. "Can I give you a hug?"

"Soon," Geraldine answered, and she went downstairs for breakfast.

Pat Hutchins

Little Pink Pig

"HURRY UP, LITTLE PINK PIG," said Little Pink Pig's mother. "It's time you were in bed."

"Wait for me," squealed Little Pink Pig.

But Little Pink Pig's mother didn't hear him.

"OINK, OINK!" cried Little Pink Pig's mother. "Where are you, Little Pink Pig?"

But Little Pink Pig couldn't hear her.

So Little Pink Pig's mother went to ask Horse if he'd seen Little Pink Pig.

"Wait for me!" squealed Little Pink Pig.

But Little Pink Pig's mother didn't hear him.

"Have you seen Little Pink Pig?" she asked Horse. "I've looked for him, and called for him, and it's time he was in bed."

Horse looked, but he couldn't see him, either.

"NEIGH!" cried Horse. "Where are you, Little Pink Pig?"

But Little Pink Pig couldn't hear him.

"Let's go and ask Cow if she's seen him," said Horse.

So off they went to look for Cow.

"Wait for me!" squealed Little Pink Pig.

But Horse and Little Pink Pig's mother didn't hear him.

"Have you seen Little Pink Pig?" they asked Cow. "We've looked for him, and called for him, and it's past his bedtime."

Cow looked, but she couldn't see him, either.

"MOO!" cried Cow. "Where are you, Little Pink Pig?"

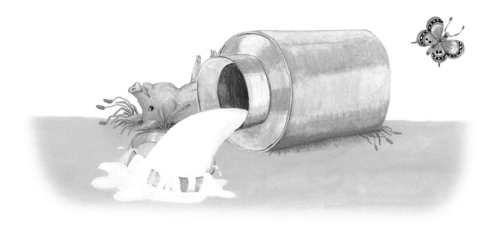

But Little Pink Pig couldn't hear her.

"Let's go and ask the sheep if they've seen him," said Cow.

So off they went to find the sheep.

"Wait for me!" squealed Little Pink Pig.

But Little Pink Pig's mother and the horse and the cow didn't hear him.

"Have you seen Little Pink Pig?" they asked the sheep. "We've looked for him, and called for him, and it's past his bedtime."

The sheep looked for
Little Pink Pig, but they
couldn't see him,
either.

"BAA!" they cried.

"Where are you, Little
Pink Pig?"

But Little Pink Pig couldn't hear them.

"Let's go and ask the hens if they've seen him," said the sheep.

So off they went to find the hens.

"Wait for me!" squealed Little Pink Pig.

But Little Pink Pig's mother and the
horse and the cow and the sheep didn't
hear him.

"Have you seen Little Pink Pig?" they asked the hens. "We've looked for him, and called for him, and it's past his bedtime."

The hens looked for Little Pink Pig, but they couldn't see him, either. "CLUCK, CLUCK!" they called. "Where are you, Little Pink Pig?"

But Little Pink Pig couldn't hear them.

Then Little Pink Pig's mother
and the horse and the cow
and the sheep and the hens
all called together.
"OINK, OINK!"
"NEIGH, NEIGH!"
"MOO, MOO!"
"BAA, BAA!"
"CLUCK, CLUCK!"
"Where are you, Little Pink Pig?"

And this time Little Pink Pig heard them.

"Here I am," he said.

"Hurry up!" said Little Pink Pig's mother. "It's past your bedtime."

"Wait for me!" squealed Little Pink Pig.

Wendy Cope

Piggies at the Party

Illustrated by Shelagh McGee

This little piggy wore trousers.
This little piggy wore a dress.
This little piggy stayed tidy.
This little piggy made a mess.

This little piggy liked the dancing.
This little piggy liked the noise.
This little piggy liked the crackers.
This little piggy liked the boys.

This little piggy passed the parcel.
This little piggy wouldn't play.
This little piggy said, "It's tea-time!"
This little piggy said, "Hooray!"

This little piggy had some ice-cream.
This little piggy had a cake.
This little piggy got sleepy.
This little piggy stayed awake.

And this little piggy had one plate of jelly,
two strawberry yogurts, three packets of
crisps, four sandwiches, five helpings of
trifle and six chocolate biscuits. And did he
go "Wee-wee-wee," all the way home? He did not.
He went "Mummy, I feel sick, Mummy" because he
had eaten far too much and, even if you're a
little piggy, that is almost always a big
mistake.

Nicholas Allan

A Pig's Book of Manners

THIS IS JOHNNY SQUELCHNOSE on his way to Lucy's party.

Here he is wishing Lucy a happy birthday.

Here he is admiring Lucy's new bike.

Here he is eating jelly without a spoon . . .

. . . and asking for cake when he hasn't finished his jelly.

Here he is after tea . . .

. . . and a little later after tea.

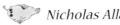

Here he is thanking
Lucy for a lovely time.

And here's Johnny Squelchnose wondering why he's not
invited to any more parties.

"You're a PIG!" said his big sister. "A PIG! That's what *you* are."

Now, just at that moment, someone new was moving in next door.

Claude Curlytail's phone never stopped ringing . . . nor did his door bell . . .

. . . and he was off to parties *every* afternoon!

But . . . he's a PIG!

. . . thought Johnny Squelchnose.

One day Claude felt so sorry for Johnny he invited him to his friend Jenny's picnic.

It was funny walking along the road with a pig, but no one seemed to notice.

When they arrived Claude said, "This is my friend Johnny."

"Hello," said Jenny.

"Grunt," said Johnny.

Claude gave Jenny a cake for the picnic.

"That Claude's *so* nice," said Jenny.

. . . whispered Johnny
Squelchnose.

Claude saw Jenny's new skateboard.

"Please, can I have a go on it – after you?" he asked.

"That Claude's *so* considerate," said Jenny.

. . . said Johnny Squelchnose.

At tea there were only two pieces of cake left. Johnny took one. Claude offered the other to Roger.

"That Claude's *so* kind," said Roger.

. . . spluttered Johnny Squelchnose.

After tea Claude helped clear up . . . while Johnny picked his nose.

"That Claude's *so* helpful," said Jenny's dad.

. . . shrieked Johnny Squelchnose.

Some time after the picnic, Claude asked, "Please, can I go to the lavatory?". . . while Johnny *didn't* ask.

"That Claude's *so* polite," said Jenny's mum.

. . . squealed Johnny Squelchnose.

BUT... slurp, slurp, snort, snort, HE'S A PIG!!

But no one listened to Johnny Squelchnose. They all wanted to be with Claude Curlytail. Until Johnny wished *he* was Claude (even if Claude *was* a pig).

So when it was time to go and Claude said, "Thanks for a lovely picnic", Johnny said . . . "Thanks for a lovely picnic, too", and everyone smiled.

"Thanks for coming," said Jenny.

Johnny felt better already.

The next day Johnny invited Claude and his friends to tea.

Johnny set the table, handed round the chocolate cake and poured the orange juice.

"What a polite boy!" beamed Mr Squelchnose.

But afterwards they played games, and got louder and *louder* and LOUDER.

Until Mr Squelchnose came storming in.

"What's all this noise?" he shouted. "You're *elephants*! ELEPHANTS! That's what you lot are!"

Just at that moment someone new was moving in – very quietly – next door.

53

Jon Blake

Wriggly Pig

Illustrated by Susie Jenkin-Pearce

THE PIGS WERE GETTING READY for their afternoon out. Mr Trevor Pig was ready. Mrs Hetty Pig was ready. Daniel Pig was ready,

and Charlotte Pig was ready. But Wriggly Pig was not ready.

"Keep still, Wriggly Pig!" said Trevor Pig, as he buttoned Wriggly's jacket.

But Wriggly Pig would not keep still.

"He should have been a worm," said Hetty Pig.

The Pigs set off in the car. Daniel Pig sat straight and looked out of the left window. Charlotte Pig sat even straighter and looked out of the right window. But Wriggly Pig fidgeted and squirmed, and tried to look out of all the windows at once.

"Keep still, Wriggly Pig!" said Hetty Pig. "I can't see the cars behind!"

But Wriggly Pig would not keep still.

"He's got ants in his pants," said Trevor Pig.

The Pigs arrived at the cinema. Soon Hetty and Trevor and Charlotte and Daniel were glued to the screen.

But Wriggly Pig was not glued to anything. He shuffled, and shifted, and rustled his popcorn.

"Keep still, Wriggly Pig!" said the goats behind. "We can't see the picture!"

But Wriggly Pig would not keep still. Soon everybody in the cinema was moaning and groaning: "Keep still, Wriggly Pig!"

The Pigs had no choice but to get up and go.

The Pigs decided to go to the beach instead. Soon Trevor and Hetty were drifting off to sleep in the warm, peaceful sun.

But Wriggly Pig could not see the point of sleeping in the middle
of the day. He tossed and turned, and sent showers
of sand all over the place.

"Keep still, Wriggly Pig!"
said Daniel Pig. "You're

getting sand in
the lunch box."

But Wriggly Pig would not keep still. There was sand in the
sandwiches, sand in the lemonade, and sand in Trevor Pig's ear.

"That's it!" said Trevor Pig. "We'll go somewhere
where there's no sand."

The Pigs arrived at the putting green. They lined up with their putters at the first hole. It was Charlotte's go first. Hetty Pig said "Ssh!" Trevor and Daniel were quiet as mice. But Wriggly Pig was not quiet. Wriggly Pig hummed and whistled, and swung with his putter.

"Keep still, Wriggly Pig!" said Charlotte Pig. "You'll put me off!"

But Wriggly Pig would not keep still. He made Charlotte so nervy, she hit her ball right over the wall. There was a loud SMASH!

"That's your fault, Wriggly Pig!" said Charlotte; and the Pigs ran as fast as they could, back to the car.

The Pigs were getting very fed up. They decided to go to a café.

It was a polite kind of café, where everyone spoke softly and sat neatly. Everyone, that is, except for Wriggly Pig. He played with the menu and tugged at the tablecloth, and scratched at his shoulderblade.

"Keep still, Wriggly Pig!" said Hetty Pig. "Everyone will think we've got fleas!"

The sheep at the next table heard Hetty say "fleas". They looked at Wriggly Pig, they looked at each other, then they got up and left.

Soon there was no one in the café but the Pigs. "That's the last straw, Wriggly Pig!" said Hetty Pig. "We're taking you to see a doctor!"

Wriggly Pig did not like the doctor's surgery. He quivered and trembled and wriggled more than usual.

"Hmm," said the doctor. "It sounds like Wriggle Fever. Or it may be Fidget-itis. I shall have to examine this pig."

Wriggly Pig did not want
to be examined.

"Keep still, Wriggly Pig!"
said the doctor, and he
pressed his cold, cold
hoofs on Wriggly's belly.

That was enough for Wriggly Pig.
He leapt off the table, dived
through the doctor's legs, and
vanished through the door.

Wriggly Pig had never run
so fast in his life. He raced
down the stairs, through
the waiting room, and
out on to the street.

He sped down the pavement
with his trotters flying,

hurtled round the corner . . .

and went BANG!
straight into a postbox.

Wriggly Pig lay very still.

"Are you all right, Wriggly Pig?" asked Hetty Pig. Wriggly Pig did not answer.

"Wake up, Wriggly Pig!" said Trevor Pig.

Wriggly did not move a muscle.

Trevor, and Hetty, and Charlotte, and Daniel began to feel very upset.

Then Wriggly's ear twitched.

His snout gave a sniff.

His tail gave a wiggle,

and his eye opened.

Soon Wriggly Pig was wriggling all over. He wriggled more than the wriggliest worm and the squirmiest snake.

The Pigs breathed a sigh of relief. They hugged Wriggly, then they hugged each other.

"From now on," said Wriggly Pig, "I really will try to keep still."

"No!" said the other Pigs. "Keep wriggling, Wriggly Pig!" And the whole family wriggled all the way home.

Errol Lloyd

Hank

Illustrated by Shelagh McGee

PLEASE
Don't call me hog
Or piglet or pig.
And if you want to be kind
Don't call me a swine.

It's true,
I have four trotters
And a snout that sticks out,
And a little tail
That curls round like a snail.
I have pink eyes too, I admit,
And large ears that flop quite a bit.
But if you want to be a friend of mine
Don't call me hog,
Piglet, pig or swine.

For I'm not flesh and blood
And I never roll in mud,
Nor do I ever grunt or squeal
For the sake of a meal.
And I never ever moan
That I can't find *my* way home.

I was bought in Brixton market
When the prices were down,
And in my belly are silver and coppers
That add up to more than a pound.
And if by now you haven't guessed,
My real name is Hank
And I am a wee wee wee piggy bank.

Susanna Gretz

Roger Mucks In!

"**W**HAT A LOVELY DAY for the beach," says Aunt Lulu.

"This is *my* seat," says Roger.

"You'll have to share it," says Uncle Tim.

Off they go.

"Oh *no*," wails Flo. "I've forgotten my bucket and spade."

"Good gravy!" says Aunt Lulu.

"You'll have to share with Roger," says Uncle Tim.

At last they arrive at the seaside.

"It's my bucket," says Roger.

"What a beautiful beach!" says Uncle Tim.

"And my spade," says Roger.

First, Roger builds a sand castle. "I need the bucket for my towers," he says.

"I need it for my river," says Flo.

"I need it and it's mine," says Roger.

Then Roger builds a village. "I need the spade for my houses," he says.

"I need it for my tunnel," says Flo.

"I need it and it's mine!" yells Roger.

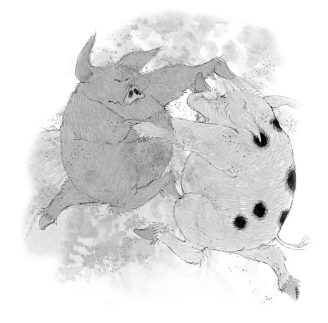

"Good gravy!" says Aunt Lulu. "Let's all go for a dip."

Then it's time for lunch.

"There's sand in my sandwich," moans Flo.

"Ha! Ha!" says Roger.

"Good gravy!" says Aunt Lulu. "Why not go exploring after lunch?"

"Right," says Roger. "Let's divide up the beach."

He draws a long line in the sand.

"This side of the line is *my* beach," he says.

He and Flo set off to explore.

Flo finds lots of sea shells, a crab's claw . . .

and an old
Wellington boot.

Roger finds some driftwood, two kinds of seaweed and some beautiful stones.

"Somebody help me!" he calls.

But Aunt Lulu is writing, Uncle Tim is reading,

and Nelson is fast asleep.

"Please!" calls Roger.

"Well . . . OK," says Flo.

"It's time to clear up," says Aunt Lulu.

"Time to muck in," says Uncle Tim.

"But that's Flo's rubbish," says Roger.

"It isn't," says Flo.

"It is," says Roger. "It's all on *your* beach, Flo."

"WHOSE beach?" roars Uncle Tim. "Listen here," he says, "it's not Flo's beach, or your beach, or our beach, or their beach, it's EVERYBODY'S beach."

"And everybody shares it," says Aunt Lulu.

So everybody, *including* Roger, mucks in.

Aunt Lulu buys them each an ice-cream cone.

"Could I borrow your boot, Flo?" Roger asks.

"Well . . ." says Flo.

At the last minute, Flo drops her ice-cream.

Oh no!

Uncle Tim looks very seriously at Roger.

"Here, Flo," says Roger, ". . . share mine."

Tony Ross

The Three Pigs

IG AND HIS TWO FRIENDS, Pig and Pig, lived on the 39th floor of a tower block. Their flat was cramped and too high, and the pigs felt sad and dizzy all the time.

"I know!" said Pig. "We'll move to the country."

"Yes!" said Pig and Pig.

The three pigs went to the Bank to borrow the money for a house but the manager wouldn't lend them any.

"We're not a *piggy bank*!" he laughed.

"I know!" said Pig. "We'll build our own houses."

"Yes!" said Pig and Pig.

The first pig met a man carrying a bundle of straw. He offered Pig some of the straw and Pig built a house with it. It wasn't strong, but it looked good and was soon finished.

But . . . a grey wolf lived near by.

As Pig made himself comfy, the wolf came to the window. He smiled a charming smile and said: *"Little pig, little pig, let me come in!"*

But Pig was too smart for that.

"No, no," he said. *"Not by the hairs of my chinny-chin-chin!"*

"*Then . . .*" roared the wolf, "*. . . I'll huff and I'll puff,
and I'll blow your house in!*"

And he *did*.

And he gobbled Pig up.

Some friendly woodcutters gave the second pig some spare sticks. "I'll build a place with these," he thought, and went to find a pleasant spot.

When the house was finished, it was stronger than the house of straw, but still not all *that* strong.

In time, the wolf came visiting.

"Little pig, little pig, let me come in!" said the wolf in a treacly voice.

But Pig was too smart for that.

"No, no," he said. "*Not by the hairs of my chinny-chin-chin!*"

"*Then . . .*" roared the wolf, ". . . *I'll huff and I'll puff, and I'll blow your house in!*"

And he *did*.

And he gobbled Pig up.

The third pig was smarter than the others. He found some help, and some bricks and cement, and built himself a real house. A strong one, with green woodwork.

In time, the grey wolf came calling.

"Little pig, little pig, let me come in!" wheedled the wolf.

"No, no," laughed Pig. *"Not by the hairs of my chinny-chin-chin!"*

"Then . . ." roared the wolf, *". . . I'll huff and I'll puff, and I'll blow your house in!"*

And he huffed and he puffed, and he coughed and he wheezed, and he strained and he roared, but the house stood firm.

So the wolf tried trickery.

"Meet me in the orchard tomorrow at six, and I'll help you collect apples," he said.

"Thank you," said Pig, and next day he went to the orchard at five.

When the wolf arrived, Pig threw apples at him. As the wolf chased the apples, Pig darted home and bolted the door. He didn't forget, of course, to take a basket full of apples with him.

The wolf called on Pig again, trying hard to smile. "I'll take you to the fair tomorrow at eight," he said.

"Thank you," said Pig, but next day he went to the fair at seven. When the wolf arrived, Pig jumped inside a milk churn to hide. The churn toppled over and clanked down the hill, straight for the terrified wolf.

When the wolf visited Pig later, he told him about the tin monster that had chased him away from the fair.

Pig laughed. "It was *me*, in my new milk churn!"

The wolf was furious, and he dropped all pretence at being the pig's friend.

Snarling and spluttering, he clawed his way on to the roof and started to wriggle down the chimney.

Pig popped his largest pan on to the fire. It was full of boiling water and spring greens.

With a snarl and a clatter, the wolf fell into the pot, and Pig slammed down the lid.

Two hours later, he gobbled the wolf up, with asparagus tips and potato croquettes.

With the wolf gone, it was quite safe to live in the country. More and more people moved from the tower blocks and built houses around Pig's house. Strong, brick houses.

Pig looked at the cramped and noisy streets. I wish I was back on the 39th floor, he thought.

Grace Nichols

Three Little Pigs

Illustrated by Shelagh McGee

THREE little pigs starting out all new
Three little pigs all wondering
    what to do
The first built a house of straw

Wolf . . . . there were two!

Two little pigs dragging their
    feet along
Two little pigs singing a sad song
The second built a house of sticks

Wolf . . . . there was one!

One little pig thinking kinda quick
One little pig saying no to straw
    and yes to brick
Built a house all sturdy and thick

Wolf . . . . huffed-puffed
    till his old jaws clicked!

Next morning the newspapers said:

CLEVER PIG GOT BAD WOLF NICKED

Sesse Koivisto

Alfred the Small

Illustrated by Anu Vanas

DEEP IN THE FOREST, where even the bright, spring sunshine found it hard to enter, lay a large mother pig. She was a wild pig and her seven, squealing, wriggling piglets were covered with stripy hair. There were three sisters and four brothers, and the smallest of them all was called Alfred.

Alfred's father was not at all little or quiet. He was a huge, black boar and he spent his days thundering about in the forest, eating sweet acorns and quarrelling with the other boars. Alfred's brothers and sisters thought he was a great hero.

At mealtimes, Alfred's brothers used to pretend that they were already grown-up like their father. They would kick and shove to get all the milk for themselves. His sisters would squeal and push and Alfred, who wanted to have his supper in peace, would get nothing at all.

He grew skinnier and quieter until even his brothers and sisters began to notice that he was different.

"Yaah! Who's the baby, then?" shouted his biggest brother.

"Alfred," laughed the others. "Alfred the small."

"Don't you call me that!" he roared; but it only came out as a squeak and his brothers and sisters laughed all the more.

One day, the teasing was even worse than usual. Alfred decided to go off exploring by himself. There must be a friendly animal somewhere, he thought miserably; someone who won't laugh at me.

Soon he came to a lake, and floating on the water was a flock of geese. How lovely they look, thought Alfred. Plucking up courage he scurried into the water squealing, "Hey! You birds! Will you be my friends?"

With a tremendous whirring of wings the geese rose indignantly into the air. They did not even bother to reply. Alfred stood still in the water, his mouth wide open with surprise and fright. Perhaps I said something wrong, he thought.

He was so busy thinking that he almost bumped into a hedgehog. The hedgehog had just woken up from his long winter sleep and he was still grumpy. "Look out! You silly little pig," he grunted.

"Sorry," said Alfred, humbly. "I was looking for a friend. Will you play with me?"

"Play?" snorted the hedgehog. "With a pig? I don't like pigs. Always doing something daft and snuffling their snouts everywhere. The cheek of it!" With that, the hedgehog rose to his feet and made for the bushes where he was soon hidden.

Alfred felt sad and ashamed. He scampered off towards the pine trees. Suddenly what looked like a dead twig wriggled in front of him. "Sstupid!" said a voice. "Watch where you're treading." It was an adder.

"Oh, dear! Oh, I am sorry!" said Alfred, in a great fright. "Please don't bite me."

The snake grinned a little. "I don't eat pigs. Even sstupid, clumsy ones like you. But what is a small piglet doing out by himself? Mmm?"

It was the first time anyone had shown any interest in him and Alfred found himself telling the adder all his problems. "I'm the littlest at home and they call me Alfred the small," he sniffed. "I just wanted to find a friend." His top lip trembled.

"Now, come along," said the adder. "None of that. I'm always on my own because people think I'm terribly poisonous. Really, I'm scared myself, a lot of the time."

"What! You scared!" said Alfred, surprised.

"Yes," said the snake, laughing, "often. But I like you, little pig. Come and talk to me again if ever you get lonely."

Alfred galloped off towards home. His tummy was empty, reminding him that breakfast had been a very long time ago. He skidded to a halt just in front of a hole in the ground. The digger appeared in a cloud of dust; a round, furry animal with large brown eyes. It was a raccoon.

"Oh, hello," she said. "Come and help me dig."

"I'd like to," said Alfred, politely, "but I'm very hungry."

"Suit yourself," said the raccoon.

"Why are you all by yourself?" asked Alfred, curiously.

"Mum is going to have some more babies," said the raccoon. "So us bigger ones have to find food for ourselves. Anyway, it was about time I was going. I rather like doing things for myself." The raccoon paused. "I'm going down to the marsh now. I know where we can find lots of sweet berries left over from the winter."

The raccoon was right. Alfred found so many berries that he forgot about going home. The moon had risen above the pine trees before he said goodbye to his new friend.

Many times throughout that spring and summer he slipped away to the marsh to play with the raccoon; digging holes, chasing through the new grass or chewing the crisp, juicy roots.

Summer came to an end and Alfred's mother began to get restless. "Autumn's here," she told her piglets. "And the hunters will soon arrive. Besides, we shall find more food deeper in the forest."

"What is autumn?" wondered the piglets. "Who are the hunters?"

One day, three men came to the forest carrying dark-coloured sticks that glinted in the autumn sunlight. "Hunters!" whispered the mother pig. "They mean death to us and the other animals in the forest. Remember that all your lives. Hurry! I told you it was time to leave."

Without another word, she set off at a quick trot, seeming not to hear her piglets' anxious whimperings. They struggled to keep up with her, too breathless even to ask questions. Alfred the small struggled hardest of all.

All of a sudden, their mother stopped. In front of them was a wide, fast-flowing river. She plunged in and the piglets splashed after her. The water was cold and Alfred felt scared. He coughed as it went up his nose. "Help!" he squealed, as the river pulled him down. He lashed out desperately; water tumbling in his ears, filling his nose, his eyes and his mouth. Then his little trotters touched the gravel at the bottom. He shook the water out of his eyes.

He was on the bank where he had started and those blurry, dark shapes were his mother and his brothers and sisters as they swam away from him across the river.

"Help! Wait!" screamed Alfred. But they had reached the other bank and

disappeared into the bushes without even a backward glance.

Alfred was so scared, he couldn't even cry. Then he calmed down a little; since meeting his friends, the adder and raccoon, he had begun to think for himself. He was cold and night was coming on: he must find shelter. Under a huge fir tree he found an ant hill and burrowed into its comforting warmth.

Soon, worn out from his adventures, his head dropped on to his little trotters and he fell fast asleep.

Morning came and the bright sunshine warmed his cold snout. He struggled out of the ant hill and set off again. He knew he must find a safe place before night came again, but where could he go?

He ran onward, eating fallen nuts and berries as he went; but something seemed different. What was it? The forest trees grew thinner and thinner and soon Alfred was in a wide meadow.

Who could have cut down all these trees? And whatever was this? Alfred was standing in front of a wooden fence. Curious, he squeezed through a little hole.

There was a warm, comforting smell and he knew it meant food. Suddenly, he heard a loud snort and a smooth, pink mother pig lumbered up, surrounded by five piglets, a few months younger than Alfred.

"Who are you, little one?" said the mother pig. "You look like a pig, even if you have got stripes."

"I'm so hungry," said Alfred, and he burst into tears.

"There, there," said the pig, kindly. "Come and have something to eat."

Gently, she let the little striped stranger join her own piglets and soon, warm and full of supper, Alfred fell peacefully asleep.

When he woke up, he told the mother pig how he had come to be alone. "Poor little pig," she said. "Stay here until the end of autumn, when we get taken inside. No one will know and you will grow big and strong. Look at you! No fat on you at all!"

The mother pig loved him as one of her own; his new brothers and sisters played with him and never took his food. In the warmth and comfort of his new family, Alfred the small began to grow plump and strong.

Then autumn passed, and Alfred was on his own again. He watched as his foster mother and brothers and sisters were taken to their winter home in the barn and he cried a little. But he was strong and well fed, his tusks had started to grow; and as he set out through the whirling leaves, he felt excited at the beginning of his new life.

Perhaps he would have felt more scared if he had known who else was in the forest. Peter Shooter was at that moment telling his friends that he was going to kill a wild boar.

Early next morning, Peter set off with his gun. He came across the prints of Alfred's sharp little trotters in the soft grass. "A young boar!" said Peter. "And he's heading for the marsh."

Quite unaware of the danger, Alfred was already nosing about for his favourite roots in the boggy earth. Peter saw him under a pine tree and he smiled. "Nearly got him!" he said. He began to creep closer, then dropped down on one knee and raised his gun.

Just at that moment, at the top of the tree, a squirrel dropped a pine cone. It clattered through the branches and hit Alfred smartly on the nose. He was terrified and shot off through the bushes – straight into Peter. It was hard to say who was the most scared. Off balance, Peter slipped in the mud and fell into a boggy pool. He scrambled out, but he had lost his gun and there was nothing for it but to go home, dripping and furious.

When he realised that he was not being chased, Alfred stopped
running. He looked up to see two birds, watching him. "Look," they said,
"that's the wild boar that sent the hunter packing. Knocked Peter's gun
clean out of his hand."

"Who? Me?" said Alfred. "I suppose I did."

From that day on, the animals thought Alfred was a hero, even if he
didn't thrash about the forest, hacking the other boars with his sharp,
new tusks. "That boar chases hunters," they would say.

And Alfred would just smile a quick proud smile and snuffle around
for another juicy root.

John Agard

Hello Moon Hello Pig

Illustrated by Shelagh McGee

THE moon
Tired of such yellowness
      such brightness
      such calmness
      such cleanness

Decided one day
To make a pig of itself

So the moon
Dipped into a puddle of mud
Rolled over on its side
In a bellyful of slush
Slobbered all its yellow
In a bed of muck

With time and practice
The moon soon had a litter
Of little yellow moons
Wallowing beside her

     And guess what?

     Someone in the heavens grunted.

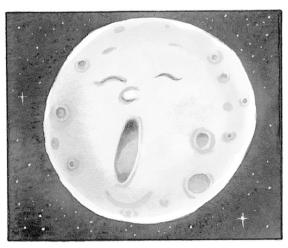

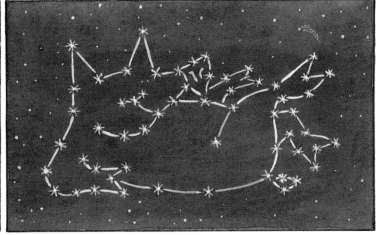

Inga Moore

The Truffle Hunter

Martine woke with a snort.
César, the chef, was in a filthy temper. "This is your last chance," he shouted, bundling her into the back of his car.

They were going truffle hunting again. Three times, now, they had been truffle hunting. Not once had she found a truffle.

"You're a dunce," César told her, "a silly sow."

Martine looked nervously out of the window. What was a truffle anyway, she wanted to know.

In the wood she darted hither and thither.

Was this a truffle? This? This? How about this then? No?

"I can't stand it!" shrieked César. He got into his car and drove off. Martine watched him bounce away without her. The twisting miles of stony road stretched out in her mind's eye. It would take ages to get home on her own.

Perhaps there was a short cut through the woods. She pushed her way into the thickets to look for one.

The woods soon turned into a great dark forest. In its depths she found a cave.

There were pictures on the walls of pigs – not dainty, domestic pigs like her, but large, hairy, wild-looking ones with long snouts and tusks.

"And how do you like my family portraits?"

Martine could hardly believe her eyes. Behind her was a pig just like the ones on the wall.

His name was Raoul. Those were his ancestors, he said.

But they weren't pigs. Neither was Raoul. He was a wild boar of the forest.

Now, being a wild boar, Raoul was very fond of truffles. In fact, he had been thinking of going out to look for some.

"I wouldn't bother," said Martine. "I've looked four times and there aren't any."

"Rubbish!" said Raoul. "You're just a dunce, that's all."

To be called a dunce twice in one day was too much for Martine.

"Well, I don't live in a damp cave," she retorted rudely, "even if it has got pictures on the wall. I have a proper tin sty with a view right across the town and my own water-dish. What's more," she went on loftily, "I ride about in a car."

Unimpressed, Raoul sniffed and rooted round under an oak tree. Suddenly he began to dig.

"There – what did I tell you?"

Martine peered into the hole at something black and wrinkled like an old potato. Was that really a truffle? No wonder they were hard to find, hiding like that under the ground. Though why anyone would want to look for one she couldn't think. Then a heavenly smell wafted up her nostrils. Her snout began to tremble and twitch. Forgetting her manners, she snapped the truffle up, drooling and gobbling.

"You nearly always find them under oak trees," she heard Raoul say helpfully, "amongst the roots."

Snout down, Martine bustled off. Sure enough, under another oak tree, she detected the same heavenly smell, faint at first, but getting stronger as she dug deep down into the earth.

And there, nestling in the roots was another truffle, black and wrinkled like before, just as delicious.

Then she found another – and another. There was no end to them. She sniffed them out and dug them up. She worked from tree to tree gorging herself.

"Come on," called Raoul at last. "Let's go down to the lake. I'm dying for a bath."

He rolled about in the mud. "This is the life," he grunted.

Martine was inclined to agree, but she said, "Oh, I don't *know*," in her haughtiest voice.

"I suppose you'll be going back soon," said Raoul, "to your precious sty and water-dish."

Martine had forgotten all about going home. Of course, now she need not return in disgrace. She would be able to show César that she *could* find truffles — and that she was not a dunce after all. He would never leave her in the woods again.

"What a proud pig," thought Raoul. Yet he couldn't help feeling sorry as he watched her set off on the long journey back to town.

Lights were going on in the houses as, trotters aching, Martine climbed the last steep steps to the hotel.

César found her next morning, snoring in her sty.

"I suppose you want another chance," he grumbled, prodding her awake.

Imagine his surprise when, in the woods, Martine began to show off her new skill. She found truffle after truffle. César dug them up and put them in his basket – truffles to put in his pâtés, his stuffings, his sauces, his seasonings.

All day, César worked in the kitchen. Martine watched the truffles disappear one by one from the basket.

Evening came. Still she waited. But not one truffle, not a sliver did César save for her.

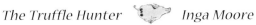

That night she looked through the dining room window at food crammed full of truffles. With a sigh she went back to her own miserable dish of scraps. Once she hadn't thought twice about cabbage stalks and potato peel. But how dreary they seemed now.

Her sty felt draughty. Its thin bed of lawn clippings was lumpy and uncomfortable.

For a while she sat looking out at the lights of the town. Then, with a kick which sent her water-dish clattering down the steps, she disappeared into the darkness.

"But what *really* brought you back to the forest?" Raoul kept asking, hoping it had been him all the time.

"Truffles," Martine insisted, though deep down, she knew it was much more.

Right from the start she'd felt at home in the forest. It was almost as if she had been there before long, long ago. And, in a way, she had. For once all pigs lived in the forest wild and free.

Like them, Martine lived a happy life. She grew a warm coat of silver hair which she kept clean and silky with plenty of mud baths. When she couldn't live on truffles she ate nuts and various kinds of roots and tubers and, in time, she had several litters of piglets.

As they grew older, she would teach her piglets to hunt truffles.

"Don't worry," she would say, if one of them was slow to learn. "It doesn't always pay to be smart."

Then she would tell them about the day she was dumped in the woods.

Roald Dahl

The Pig

Illustrated by Quentin Blake

IN England once there lived a big
And wonderfully clever pig.
To everybody it was plain
That Piggy had a massive brain.
He worked out sums inside his head,
There was no book he hadn't read,
He knew what made an airplane fly,
He knew how engines worked and why.
He knew all this, but in the end
One question drove him round the bend:
He simply couldn't puzzle out
What LIFE was really all about.
What was the reason for his birth?
Why was he placed upon this earth?

His giant brain went round and round.

Alas, no answer could be found,

Till suddenly one wondrous night,

All in a flash, he saw the light.

He jumped up like a ballet dancer

And yelled, "By gum, I've got the answer!

"They want my bacon slice by slice

"To sell at a tremendous price!

"They want my tender juicy chops

"To put in all the butchers' shops!

"They want my pork to make a roast

"And that's the part'll cost the most!

"They want my sausages in strings!

"They even want my chitterlings!

"The butcher's shop! The carving knife!
"That is the reason for my life!"
Such thoughts as these are not designed
To give a pig great peace of mind.
Next morning, in comes Farmer Bland,
A pail of pigswill in his hand,
And Piggy with a mighty roar,
Bashes the farmer to the floor . . .
Now comes the rather grizzly bit
So let's not make too much of it,

Except that you *must* understand

That Piggy *did eat* Farmer Bland,

He ate him up from head to toe,

Chewing the pieces nice and slow.

It took an hour to reach the feet,

Because there was so much to eat,

And when he'd finished, Pig, of course,

Felt absolutely no remorse.

Slowly he scratched his brainy head

And with a little smile, he said,

"I had a fairly powerful hunch

"That he might have me for his lunch.

"And so, because I feared the worst,

"I thought I'd better eat *him* first."

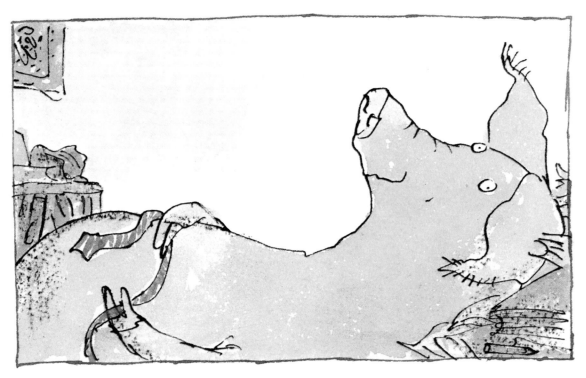

ACKNOWLEDGEMENTS

THE PUBLISHERS GRATEFULLY ACKNOWLEDGE THE FOLLOWING
AUTHORS AND ILLUSTRATORS:

Text and illustrations from *Boo!* copyright © 1995, 1996 by Colin McNaughton,
reprinted with permission of Andersen Press and Harcourt, Inc.

Geraldine's Baby Brother copyright © 1994 by Holly Keller, used by permission
of Julia MacRae Books and HarperCollins Publishers

Little Pink Pig copyright © 1994 by Pat Hutchins, used by permission
of Julia MacRae Books and HarperCollins Publishers

'Piggies at the Party' from *Piggy Poems* published by The Bodley Head Children's Books
© text Wendy Cope 1992, reproduced by permission of the author
© illustrations Shelagh McGee 1992

A Pig's Book of Manners published by Hutchinson Children's Books
© Nicholas Allan 1995

Wriggly Pig published by Hutchinson Children's Books
© text Jon Blake 1991 © illustrations Susie Jenkin-Pearce 1991

'Hank' from *Piggy Poems* published by The Bodley Head Children's Books
© text Errol Lloyd 1992, reproduced by permission of the author
© illustrations Shelagh McGee 1992

Roger Mucks In! published by The Bodley Head Children's Books
© Susanna Gretz 1989

The Three Pigs published in a fully illustrated edition by Andersen Press
© Tony Ross 1983

'Three Little Pigs' from *Piggy Poems* published by The Bodley Head Children's Books
© text Grace Nichols 1992, reproduced with permission of Curtis Brown Ltd, London,
on behalf of Grace Nichols © illustrations Shelagh McGee 1992

Alfred the Small published by Hutchinson Children's Books
© text Sesse Koivisto 1987 © translation Hutchinson Children's Books 1988
© illustrations Anu Vanas 1987

'Hello Moon Hello Pig' from *Piggy Poems* published by The Bodley Head Children's Books
© text John Agard 1992, reproduced by kind permission of the author
c/o Caroline Sheldon Literary Agency
© illustrations Shelagh McGee 1992

The Truffle Hunter published in a fully illustrated edition by Andersen Press
© Inga Moore 1985

'The Pig' from *Dirty Beasts* published by Jonathan Cape and Farrar, Straus & Giroux, Inc.
© text Roald Dahl Nominee Ltd 1983, reprinted by permission
of the publishers and David Higham Associates
© illustrations Quentin Blake 1984, reproduced by permission of the
publishers and AP Watt, Ltd, London, on behalf of Quentin Blake

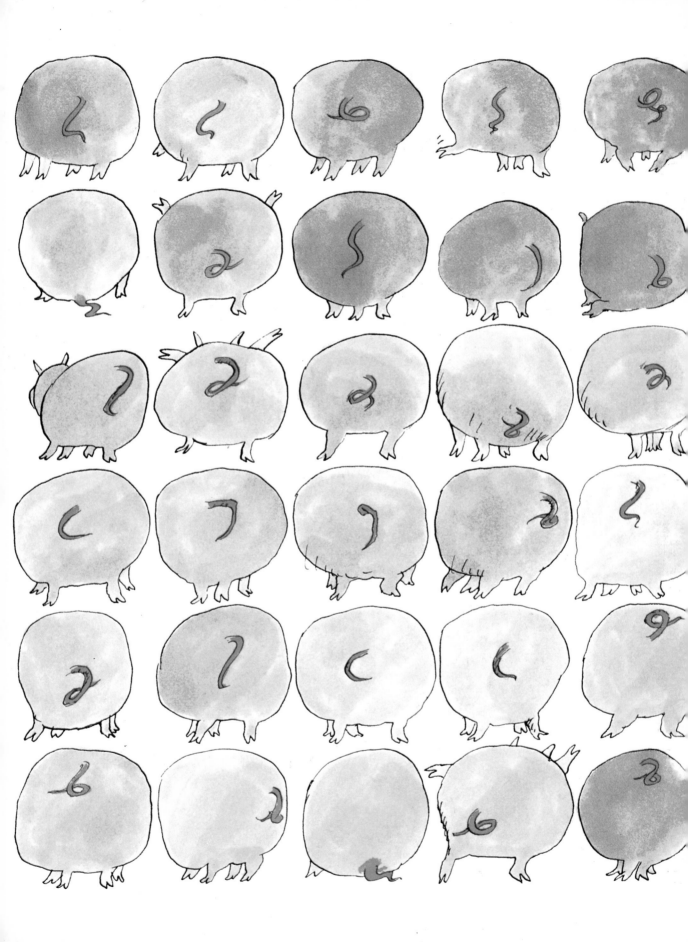